"Me nt," Mr. Slocum began. "The league has just told me that we're going to have a new forward playing for us for the rest of the season. Someone who just moved to town this year. I think a few of you might know her. Sari Baxter."

There was total silence for about one second. Then everyone started shouting at once.

"A girl!"

"No way. I'll quit!"

"You've got to be kidding."

"Girls aren't allowed in *our* league."

The No Stars need all the fans they can get!

So don't miss:

#1 STICKING IT OUT

#2 THE PUCK STOPS HERE!

And coming soon:

#3 CALL ME GRETZKY!

#4 LET'S HEAR IT FOR THE SHRUMPS!

1

STICKING IT OUT

By Jim O'Connor

Bullseye Books
Random House New York

The No Stars™ are created by Parachute Press, Inc.

Ice hockey equipment provided by CANSTAR Sports, Inc., makers of Bauer and Cooper hockey equipment and ice skates.

A BULLSEYE BOOK PUBLISHED BY RANDOM HOUSE, INC.

Published in the United States by Random House, Inc., New York, and simultaneously in Canada by Random House of Canada Limited, Toronto.

Library of Congress Catalog Card Number: 95-70654
ISBN: 0-679-87858-0
RL: 2.1

Manufactured in the United States of America 10 9 8 7 6 5 4 3 2 1

CONTENTS

I can't explain how it happened. It was like a bad dream. A nightmare, really.

The North Stars, my hockey team, were playing the Red Wings. The score was tied 2–2. It was our best game this season.

We had already lost our first three games. And I mean lost them *bad!* First the Penguins shut us out, 11–0. Then the Black Hawks beat us, 5–1. Our last game started out great. We scored three goals right away. But the Islanders got seven in a row and beat us.

So this tie was looking good. Real good.

My name is Mike Beagleman. I'm nine years old and in the fourth grade. My dad's a high school history teacher. My mom sells houses. I don't have any brothers or sisters. But I do have a dog named Ranger. That's because the New York Rangers are my favorite team. I love hockey more than anything in the world.

I live in Monroeville, Wisconsin, where hockey's a big deal. Almost every kid in town is in a league. There's the Westside League and the Eastside League. The North Stars are in the Westside League.

At the end of every season, the number-one team in each league plays for the Monroeville Hockey Association Championship. It's called the Mayor's Cup, because the mayor gives a really cool silver trophy cup to the winning team. They write the team's name on the side. They even take your picture and put it on the front page of the Monroeville *Times-Union*.

This is my third year on the North Stars, and we've never even come close to first place. Two years ago we were 8–8. Last year we won five games. And lost eleven. It looks as if we're getting *worse* instead of better!

In fact, some kids have started calling us the *No* Stars instead of the *North* Stars because we're so bad. My mom tells me to not let stuff like that bother me. But it does.

Last season, the Penguins won the Cup. They've been acting like jerks ever since. They go around yelling "Penguins rule!" everywhere. They even do it in the halls at school!

I wanted to show them they weren't so great. That's why even a tie would be a step up. And maybe, just maybe, we had a shot at a win.

Teddy Ryan, Lucas Wilson, and I were playing the forward line. Guys on the line are supposed to score goals. Cliff Parkes and Felipe Perez were playing defense.

One of the Red Wings took a shot at our goal. But Cliff blocked the puck. Cliff just moved to Monroeville last summer. He's the newest player on the team. And the biggest. I also think he's the nicest. Cliff has dark black eyes, light brown skin, and a loud laugh. My dad calls him "The Gentle Giant." Cliff never played hockey before. But he's learning fast.

Now he was skating up ice with the puck.

"Cliff! Cliff!" I heard Felipe yell. Felipe wanted the puck. He always wants the puck. He's our captain. Felipe is tall and skinny and likes to tell everyone what to do during a game. We don't usually mind, because he's the fastest skater on the team.

Cliff had his head down, pushing the puck in front of him. *Swish, swish, swish* went his skates. Cliff is pretty fast once he gets going.

He does have one problem. Stopping.

Cliff just can't seem to get the hang of it. So when he wants to slow down, he grabs on to whoever happens to be nearby. It's not too bad when it's one of the North Stars. But sometimes Cliff grabs someone on the other team. Then he usually gets called for a penalty.

I spotted a Red Wing getting set to knock the puck away from Cliff. "Pass it!" I hollered.

I don't know if Cliff heard me, but just then he slid the puck across the ice to Felipe. *Yes!* Beautiful pass.

"Felipe, watch out!" I heard Lucas yell. A Red Wing was skating up behind Felipe.

But I could tell Felipe was going to hang on to that puck. He wanted to make the score himself.

I can't really blame him. He hasn't

scored once this season. And I know it bugs him, because last year he made the most goals for our team. So there was no way Felipe was going to pass the puck.

Felipe swerved so hard to his left that a big spray of ice chips flew into the air. The Red Wing sailed right by Felipe and crashed into the sideboards. Felipe's smile was so big I could see it behind the cage of his helmet. But just then another Red Wing ran right into him.

Felipe flew in one direction. His stick went in another. And the puck sailed straight to me.

"Go for it, Mike!" I heard Mr. Slocum, our coach, yell from the bench.

This was my chance!

"Give and go," I shouted to Teddy. It's a play we'd worked on all week. I take the puck into the opposing team's zone and then pass it to Teddy. Then I head for the net. When I was in position, Teddy would pass it back to me. I could take a shot or pass it again.

If everything went right, it would be an easy goal. Easy!

But when I skated with the puck, Teddy and Lucas didn't move.

"Come on!" I yelled. What was wrong with them?

"Mike, Mike!" Mr. Slocum's voice shot across the ice.

I zoomed on. Right past Felipe. Right past Cliff. They were screaming my name, too.

I had never skated better. The puck seemed glued to my stick. No Red Wing even came close. I pushed the puck a little harder and brought my stick back for a shot.

"No, Mike, no!" I heard Felipe yell.

He's jealous, I thought. *Well, too bad. This one's mine!*

I hit the puck as hard as I could. I

watched it fly by the goalie.

Our goalie.

In one terrible moment it hit me. I had skated *the wrong way!*

No wonder Teddy and Lucas hadn't followed me.

No wonder Felipe had yelled at me.

No wonder none of the Red Wings had tried to stop me.

I heard the buzzer go off. The game was over. My heart sank into my stomach.

I had just scored the winning goal. For the other team.

I opened my mouth to say something. But no words came out. I just stared at our goalie, Steve Slocum. He stared back.

The Red Wings were falling all over themselves laughing. "He scored on his own goalie!" their captain yelled. I wanted to disappear.

Steve poked the puck out of the net with his stick. It hit my skate and stopped. I hated that puck. I wanted to hit it so hard that it would blast through the walls and disappear into outer space. Just like a cartoon.

I was still thinking about sending the puck into orbit when the referee skated over.

"Too bad, guys," he said. "Better luck next time." He picked up the puck and skated away.

Steve glared at me and then glided right past me without a word. He was really mad.

I didn't think it was fair for him to be so mad. He's not such a great goalie. Some guys on the team call him "Steve the Sieve" because he lets so many goals slide in. I never called him that. Even though it's true.

I skated really slowly over to the bench. My eyes were a little teary, and I had a lump in my throat the size of that dumb puck. I could feel the redness in my cheeks. Teddy stood there, waiting for me. He was the only one.

"Tough break," Teddy said. Teddy and I

don't go to the same school or even live in the same neighborhood. But we've played together on the North Stars for three years, and we're best friends. So I knew he felt bad for me.

Teddy is one of our top players. It's weird, because he's not the fastest skater. He's not big, either. In fact, he's shorter than everyone except Brendan Murphy, our backup goalie. And Teddy wears glasses all the time. Without them, he can't see a thing. Teddy doesn't have a great shot like Felipe. But he always seems to be in the right place during a game. And he never makes a mistake.

Teddy and I walked into the locker room. Most of the guys were already changing into their street clothes and sneakers. When Steve saw me, he turned away. What a jerk.

"Tough game, men," Mr. Slocum said. I hate it when he calls us "men."

"Mike, don't get down on yourself." Mr. Slocum clapped a hand on my shoulder. "You were going for a win. Good for you."

I glanced over at Steve. Mr. Slocum is his dad. I knew that Steve would be mad that his dad didn't yell at me for scoring that goal.

"Sure, we've had some bad luck," Mr. Slocum continued, pacing in a circle. "But what do we say? 'When the going gets tough…'"

"'The tough get going,'" we all mumbled. Mr. Slocum has about a thousand stupid sayings like that. Lucas says that Mr. Slocum probably has a list of things coaches are supposed to say taped to his refrigerator door. Like "There's no 'I' in team" and "Winners never quit and quitters never win." Let me tell you, those slogans get boring after a while.

Especially when you aren't winning any games.

"Men," Mr. Slocum went on, "don't forget our next practice. It's at six A.M. sharp on Saturday morning. Last man here has to skate extra laps after practice."

Mr. Slocum glanced at his watch. "I want everybody to stay a few more minutes. I have to check on something. Then I may have a big announcement."

"I'll go with you, Dad," Steve piped up. I guess he didn't want to be in the same room with me.

After Mr. Slocum and Steve left, the locker room became very quiet. No one wanted to say anything. But I knew Felipe wouldn't be able to keep his mouth shut for long.

And I was right.

"Nice shot, Mike," Felipe said. "I know how tough it is to score on Steve the Sieve."

Felipe laughed at his own joke. Then Cliff started giggling. I gazed around.

Everyone was grinning.

"Very funny, you guys." I could feel my face turning red again. Even worse, my eyes started to get that stinging feeling again.

"Don't feel bad, Mike," Cliff said. "Remember the first time I played hockey? I didn't know how to stop. So I flipped right over the boards. I was so embarrassed I wanted to move right back to Arizona."

"Or how about our first game with the Penguins," Teddy said. "I forgot one of my skates. My mom had to go all the way home and get it. I missed the whole first period!"

Then everybody started talking and laughing at once. Tommy Feldman admitted he called the puck "the ball" during his first practice. And Randy Fernandez claimed that he once saw Steve pick his nose during a game.

"I swear it's true!" Randy said. "Steve

took his glove off and was really digging around up there. When the Islanders came down on a breakaway, Steve's whole hand was stuck behind his face mask. It was the easiest goal they ever scored!"

"No way," Cliff said. "You're making that up."

"I am not," said Randy. "Ask anyone. It happened. Really!"

Lucas picked up his stick and held the end of it up to his mouth like a microphone. Then he started talking like an announcer on TV.

"We're interviewing Mike Beagleman of the Westside North Stars. Tell us, Mike. You've seen a lot of amazing things happen in your career. Were you there the day Steve 'the Sieve' Slocum picked his nose?"

I was laughing so hard I could hardly talk. To tell the truth, I didn't remember Steve doing anything that gross. But I didn't want to ruin Lucas's act.

Lucas has had a rough year. His mom and dad separated during the summer. Now he lives with his dad on weekends and his mom during the week. He hardly ever smiles anymore. So I was happy to play along.

"Well, Lucas..." I pretended to speak into the end of his hockey stick. "I guess Steve showed us a move we never saw before."

Lucas opened his mouth to say something, but suddenly his eyes got really wide. He was staring at something behind me.

I turned around. It was Steve. He and his dad had just walked back into the locker room. From the look on Steve's face, he had definitely heard me.

Before Steve could sock me, his dad started talking. "Men, I have an announcement," Mr. Slocum began. "The league has just told me that we're going to have a new player for the rest of the season. Someone who just moved to town this year. I think a few of you might know her. Sari Baxter."

There was total silence for about one second. Then everyone started shouting at once.

"A girl!"

"No way. I'll quit!"

"You've got to be kidding."

"Girls aren't allowed in *our* league."

Mr. Slocum held up his hands. "Hold on, hold on. I know you're surprised, but this will be good for the team. First of all, girls *are* allowed in our league. It's just that Sari is the first girl who tried out."

"Girls stink!" Randy yelled.

"I saw her at a clinic for new players last week," Mr. Slocum went on. "She's a very fast skater and has a really good shot."

"But why does she have to play for us?" Felipe asked. "The rest of the teams are already laughing at us because we're so bad. If we have a girl, they'll never let up."

"Sari's playing for us because we're the only team that has a spot open," Mr. Slocum said. "It's as simple as that."

"Well, I'm not playing with any girl," Felipe announced. He crossed his arms and glared. He looked as if he meant it.

"I can't make you play with Sari," Mr. Slocum said quietly. "But I will tell you this. No one had better think about quitting the North Stars over this. If you do, you won't be able to play again. No other team in the league will take you. And remember, men, 'Winners never quit.'"

"'And quitters never win,'" we all mumbled glumly.

"I'm expecting a positive attitude about Sari, men. Give her a chance," Mr. Slocum told us. "Practice is at six A.M. Saturday.

That's when you'll meet your new teammate."

I guessed if there was a girl on the team, Mr. Slocum would at least stop calling us "men."

But that really didn't make me feel better. We had the worst team in the league. Plus a goalie who couldn't block the puck. And at least three guys who were still learning how to skate.

And now, we were going to have the only girl in the entire league.

Great. Just great.

B*leeep! Bleeep!* My alarm blasted me awake. I peered at the clock. The numbers 5:15 glowed in the dark.

It was Saturday. Hockey practice started at six A.M. I loved Saturday morning practice. It was a great way to start the day.

I jumped out of bed and started to get dressed. All my hockey gear was laid out on the chair. I pulled my favorite hockey jersey over my head. Then I remembered that today's practice was going to be different. Today was Sari Baxter's first practice with our team.

I hoped it would be her last.

I already kind of knew Sari. She's in the other fourth-grade class at Vince Lombardi Elementary School. That's where Felipe, Cliff, Randy, and I all go.

Sari was new this year. New kids always stand out. I'd seen her walking around, but I never talked to her. I heard she was a really good soccer player.

But Sari didn't look like she would be much of a hockey player. She's kind of skinny. I was sure she wouldn't last one whole practice. That cheered me up.

My dad dropped me off at the rink at five minutes to six. Everybody was already out on the ice. Mr. Slocum stood by the bench at the side of the rink with his clipboard.

"Hurry up, Mike," he called. "You're the last one here. Remember what I said—extra laps after practice for the last man."

This wasn't going to be my day.

But then I realized something. There were no new skaters. Sari Baxter hadn't shown up!

"I guess she chickened out," I said to Cliff when I got on the ice.

"Why would she try out for a team if she wasn't going to show up?" Cliff asked me.

"Like I said, she's a chicken," I explained. "She knows she'll be laughed off this rink. No way a girl can play hockey."

Of course, that was when Sari Baxter stepped onto the ice. She was wearing big black hockey skates—a kid's version of the skates most pros wear. They were really cool. She had on a complete hockey outfit—padded shorts, and arm, leg, and shoulder pads, and a black helmet with a black cage. She wore an old gray sweatshirt with MAINE HOCKEY on the front.

Sari started skating in a big circle. No

one said hello or hi or anything like that.

Lucas and Felipe skated up behind me and Cliff.

"Look at that," Felipe sneered. "Her mother brought her to practice."

"What's so weird about that?" Cliff asked Felipe. "My mom drives me here all the time."

Before Felipe could answer, Mr. Slocum blew his whistle to signal the start of practice. We all skated over to the bench and sat down. Everyone crowded together. Sari had to sit all the way at one end of the bench by herself.

"Okay, let's quiet down," Mr. Slocum said. "First, I'd like everyone to say hi to Sari Baxter. She's joining the North Stars today."

No one said a word. Mr. Slocum studied his clipboard for a couple of seconds. When he looked back up at us, he wasn't smiling.

"Okay, that's that," he said. "Now, let's start with some passing drills."

He pointed to the end of the bench. "Sari, you'll skate with Tommy and Randy."

I glanced over at them. Tommy and Randy didn't look happy. "Sure, Coach," Sari said.

Coach! No one ever calls Mr. Slocum "Coach." She must have been trying to get on his good side. That way, he wouldn't kick her off the team when he saw how bad she was.

"Okay, men, hit the ice," Mr. Slocum said.

Men? I guess Mr. Slocum was having trouble getting used to having a girl on the team, too.

I lined up with Teddy and Lucas for the passing drill. Tommy, Randy, and Sari skated first. Randy passed the puck to Tommy, who was in the center of the line. Then Tommy passed to Sari on the left wing. She took two steps and sent a perfect pass all the way back across the rink to Randy. He flipped the puck into the net.

Then it was our turn. Lucas had the puck, Teddy played center, and I was on left wing.

We had trouble right away. Lucas's pass missed Teddy completely. So I had to race to get the puck before it hit the boards.

My pass back to Teddy was way off. Lucas tried to stop it, but the puck hit the tip of his blade. It skidded past him.

"That pass really stunk," he snarled at me.

"What are you talking about?" I cried. "You missed Teddy completely!"

"Well, so did you!" Lucas shot back.

"Cut it out, you guys," Teddy whispered. "She'll hear you."

I glanced over at Sari, Tommy, and Randy. Sari was watching our every move.

The next couple of tries, we did better.

Not great, but better. But whenever Sari, Randy, and Tommy were on the ice, they looked as if they had played together all year. Every pass was perfect.

Sari was a very good skater. She moved with long, powerful glides. And she was fast, just as Mr. Slocum had said.

Mr. Slocum changed the drill—skating backward. If you can't skate backward, you can't play good defense. I'm getting better at it, but I still lose my balance and fall on my rear a lot.

Felipe's great at skating backward. But Sari was better.

Then Mr. Slocum blew his whistle. "Okay, men. Take a water break. We'll finish with a practice game."

"Guys, over here. I've got an idea," Felipe said when we came back from the drinking fountain. We all gathered around him.

"Maybe Sari can skate. And her passing's pretty good. But she's still a girl," Felipe whispered. "If we check her hard, she'll give up. One good hip check and I bet she's out of here."

"You're right," Lucas said. "Good idea."

"Why don't you leave Sari alone?" Randy said to Felipe. "She's good. You know, she's better than a couple of the guys on this team."

"What's going on, Randy?" Felipe asked. "You skate with her for twenty minutes, and now Sari's your best friend? Or maybe she's your *girlfriend?*"

Randy just rolled his eyes at Felipe.

"Sometimes you're such an idiot," Tommy said to Felipe. "You know she can help the team. Sari *is* better than some of us. She's sure faster than I am. Why is it such a big deal to you, anyway?"

Felipe didn't answer Tommy. He just skated to the center of the ice, waiting for the practice game to start.

I didn't know what to think. Sari *was* good, but I still didn't want her on the team. But knocking her down? Wasn't that going too far?

Mr. Slocum split us into two teams. Sari, Randy, and Tommy were on one team. They took the puck first. Lucas, Teddy, and I were on the other team. We had to try to stop them. Felipe and Cliff were our defense.

As Sari came down the ice, I could tell that Lucas was all set to hip-check her. But Sari saw him coming. She surprised him by skating backward. With the puck! Lucas was totally fooled. He missed Sari and crashed into the boards.

"What are you doing, Lucas?" Mr. Slocum shouted. He shook his head.

Then Sari took off. She buzzed down the rink. She guarded the puck with the blade of her stick. I turned around and skated after her as hard as I could. Sari tried to pass it to Randy. But I got the puck instead. I made a perfect pass back to Lucas.

There was no one between Lucas and the goal.

But Sari didn't give up. In a flash, she skated right by me. She was going so fast her long blond ponytail flew straight out behind her.

She caught up with Lucas. And stole the puck from him. She turned around toward the other end of the ice, flew by me, and took a shot at the goal.

But our goalie was ready for it. He knocked the puck away with his stick. It landed right in front of Felipe. He tried one of his favorite tricks—a flip pass. The puck was supposed to go over Sari's head to me or Teddy.

But it hit Sari right in the face mask with a loud *thwack!* I saw her head snap back. I thought she would fall down or at least stop. Getting hit in the face can really shake you up.

But when the puck dropped to the ice, Sari shot it right back at the net. She didn't even flinch! Instead, she scored a goal.

When Mr. Slocum blew his whistle to end practice, everyone rushed to get a drink of water.

"Nice game," Sari said to Felipe.

Felipe spat a mouthful of water onto the floor. He just missed hitting Sari's foot. "Why don't you take a hint?" he sneered. "No one wants a girl on the team."

"What makes you think being on your team is such a big deal?" Sari answered back. "You guys are a bunch of wimpy, whiny losers."

"Okay, cut it out," Mr. Slocum said. "Keep fighting, and you'll both skate extra laps."

Then Mr. Slocum spotted me. "That reminds me. Mike, you were the last to arrive. You owe me four laps around the rink."

"I wasn't last," I said. "Sari was."

"Nice try, Mike. But Sari doesn't count this time. She's new. She didn't know about the rule."

"But, Mr. Slocum, that's not fair..."

"It's only four laps now, Mike," Mr. Slocum said. "Do you want me to make it five?"

"Okay, okay," I grumbled. I headed back out onto the ice and started skating. My legs felt like jelly. I was really tired.

By my second lap, no one was left on the bench. I could see Sari and her mother standing by the door. Her mom had her arm around Sari's shoulders. She seemed to be whispering something to her.

Maybe she's talking her into quitting, I thought hopefully. *Maybe she'll explain that the other teams will make fun of us. That we're already the joke of the league.*

But then I heard them both laugh. And I knew that, for now, Sari was still on our team.

Great. Just great.

Tights and Tutus

Monday was the worst day of my life. And it was all Sari Baxter's fault.

It started the minute I got to school. I was walking down the hall toward my homeroom when someone yelled my name.

"Yo, Beagleman. Tell me it's not true!"

It was Rick Gates. He's the goalie for the Penguins and a real pain. Lucas calls him "Thick Rick" because he acts so dumb.

"What are you talking about, Rick?" I asked. But I had a sick feeling I already knew. Somehow he must have heard about Sari Baxter.

"Sari what's-her-face," Rick sneered. "That girl on your team. You No Stars must really be hard up." He laughed.

"It wasn't our idea," I protested. "The league made us take her. It's a new rule."

"Sure, Beagleman, sure," Rick said. "Hey, Tony, come here! I've got something to tell you."

Rick was waving at Tony Kelley. He's the captain of the Penguins. A lot of people think Tony is the coolest kid in our school. He's a really good athlete and smart. And some of the girls think he's cute. Whatever that means.

Tony and Rick slapped high-fives and yelled, "Penguins rule!" They were really loud.

"What's up?" Tony asked Rick. He pretended I wasn't even there.

"The No Stars have a new player," Rick

said, grinning from ear-to-ear.

"Big deal," Tony said.

"It's Sari Baxter!" Rick shouted as loud as he could. About six kids turned around and looked at him.

"A girl!" Tony hollered back. More kids turned around. Pretty soon the whole school would be staring at us.

"I knew you guys were hopeless," Tony said to me. "But bringing a girl into our hockey league? That...that's pathetic."

"It wasn't *our* idea," I said again. "The league's making us."

"They'd never be able to make the Penguins take a girl," Tony boasted. "I just hope you guys don't come to the game Wednesday night wearing tights and tutus."

"Good one, Tony," Rick said with a laugh. They slapped high-fives again and started down the hall. When they were about five feet away, they turned and yelled "Byyye, Mikeyyy," in really high, girlish voices.

I clapped my hand to my forehead. I'd completely forgotten that our next game was against the Penguins. We already lost to them once this season, 11–0. Now we had to play them again. This time with Sari Baxter. What a disaster.

I hurried into homeroom and raced over to Cliff's desk. He was reading a book. He loves to read.

He shut the book and looked up at me. "What's up?" he asked.

"I just ran into Thick Rick and Tony Kelley," I explained. I tried to stay calm. "They know about Sari being on our team. You can bet everyone else in school knows, too."

Before I could say another word, our teacher, Mrs. Nagan, came in and class started. But I couldn't listen. All I could think about was how the whole school would know that Sari Baxter was on the North Stars. We would get a lot of grief.

Sometimes I hate being right.

When Felipe, Cliff, Randy, and I went to the cafeteria for lunch, about ten different guys came over and made cracks.

"Yo, Randy. I hear you have new pink uniforms."

"Oh, Cliffy! I love your hair!"

"Very funny," Cliff muttered. It was even starting to get to him. And it takes a lot to get Cliff mad.

"Hey, Felipe!" It was Thick Rick. He was standing with some of the other Penguins. "Is it true that you guys are having a pajama party after the game? Are you going to play with your dolls?"

That's when Felipe totally lost it. He shot across the cafeteria in a flash. He wrestled Rick into a headlock.

"What did you say?" Felipe demanded.

One of the teachers ran over and separated them. I don't know what she said to them, but Felipe and Rick shook hands. But they didn't look as if they really meant it.

"We've got to do something," Felipe said when he came back to our table.

"Like what?" Randy asked.

"Like get Sari to quit the team, that's what," Felipe replied.

"Well, count me out," Randy said. "She's the best center I've ever played with. These guys will shut up once they see her play."

"You're wrong!" Felipe snapped. "They'll never let up."

"Don't look at me!" Cliff said. "I don't want to talk to her."

Felipe turned to me. "Mike, it's up to you."

"Me? Why me?" I asked.

"You're the only one left," Felipe answered. "And now's your chance. There she is." Felipe pointed across the lunchroom. "Go talk to her."

I glanced over. Sari was sitting at a table with some other girls. "She, uh, she looks busy," I said. I didn't want to do this. Not in front of the whole lunchroom.

But Felipe had other ideas. He practically shoved me out of my chair. "We're counting on you, Mike," Felipe said. "Go get her."

I walked over to the table. I felt as if everybody in school were watching me. All the girls stopped talking.

"Sari, can I, uh, can I talk to you for a second?"

"Sure, Mike. What's up?"

I gazed around the table. All the girls sat there, their big eyes fixed on me. Some started giggling.

"Can we go out in the hall? It's kind of private. You know. It's about the North Stars."

"No problem," she said.

We walked out into the hall. I wanted to get this over with fast. I just hoped she wouldn't cry.

"Sari," I began, "it's about the team. I know you think that we don't want you to play with us. But that's not it. It's not us. It's the other teams. They can be really mean. So we think it would be better for you if you didn't play."

That sounded good. As if I was looking out for *her*.

Sari didn't say anything. She nodded her head a couple of times. I figured that meant she got my point.

"So, anyhow," I finished, "if you really think about what I'm saying, uhm. Ah." I was running out of steam. "I think... Ah...you'll agree that not playing for the North Stars would be the smart thing for you to do. Everyone would understand. No one would make fun of you for quit—I mean, for not playing. Okay?"

Sari had a strange look on her face. At least she wasn't crying. "Hmmm. Okay," she said. "Thanks. I guess I'll see you around."

So that was it. Done! I backed away from her down the hall. "Bye," she called after me.

I scooted back into the lunchroom and over to our table. The guys were all waiting for me.

"How did it go?" Felipe asked. Felipe, Cliff, and Randy stared at me. Waiting.

"It was easy," I said. "She agreed with everything I said."

Things were definitely looking up.

Puck Hogs

I hate being wrong.

As soon as I got to the rink Wednesday night for the game with the Penguins, Felipe grabbed me.

"Whoa!" I said. "What's with you?"

"Take a look," Felipe growled. He pointed me toward the ice.

"What is *she* doing here?" I moaned. Sari Baxter was gliding around the rink with smooth, strong strides. She wore a brand-new purple-and-black North Stars jersey.

"I thought you talked her into quitting!" Felipe said.

"I did! At least, she sure seemed like she was agreeing with me." Girls. You just can't trust them.

Felipe didn't say another word. He climbed over the boards and started skating around the rink.

The Penguins were at the other end of the rink, warming up. One by one our guys arrived and got onto the ice.

I had just passed a puck to Teddy when Lucas skated over to me.

"I thought you were going to talk her out of this," he said.

"I thought I had," I said, glancing across the ice at Sari.

Lucas turned and skated away. I could see him shaking his head. Now I was getting annoyed. Why was everyone blaming me?

Then Mr. Slocum called the whole team

over to the bench.

"Okay, North Stars. Listen up," he said. "I'm switching lines around tonight."

Mr. Slocum looked at us and took a deep breath. "Randy, Tommy, and Sari are the first line. Sari, I want you to play center. Then Mike, Lucas, and Teddy on the second line. The defense doesn't change."

I couldn't believe my ears. Sari was centering the first line. Ahead of Lucas! The first line was supposed to have the best players.

I glanced at Lucas. He looked furious. His face was bright red.

"Okay, men," Mr. Slocum said. "I want you to forget about the last time we played the Penguins. We've improved a lot. Think positive! We can beat these guys."

Then we formed a circle and each put one hand in the middle. "Gooooooo, NORTH STARS!" we shouted. Sari yelled the loudest.

Tony Kelley centered the Penguins' first line. When the referee dropped the puck, Sari's stick slashed out and hit it back to Randy. Tony's mouth dropped open. Sari was really quick.

Randy, Tommy, and Sari took off with the puck. The Penguins were caught totally by surprise.

Randy sent the puck over to Tommy. He took it around behind the Penguins' goal. When he came out the other side, Sari was standing about five feet in front of the net.

Tommy's pass sailed right to her. In a flash, Sari shot the puck into the net. Goal!

The North Stars side of the stands went crazy. Sari's parents jumped up and down, hugging each other. My dad rang the cowbell he brings to all the games. All of us on the bench screamed and shouted. Everyone except Lucas and Felipe.

"Next line," Mr. Slocum called.

Teddy, Lucas, and I hurried onto the ice. Sari had scored so fast that the Penguin coach left Tony's line out there for another shift.

I guess Teddy couldn't help it. "Hey, Tony, beat by a *girl*," Teddy taunted.

"Shut up," Tony said. He sounded really mad.

As soon as the referee dropped the puck, Tony knocked Teddy down. He didn't even pretend to go for the puck.

The referee called a penalty on Tony. Teddy limped off the ice. Tony must have hit him hard.

"Sit down, Teddy. You'll feel better in a couple of minutes," Mr. Slocum said. "Okay, men, this is our chance. We have one more player than they do. Let's get our best shots out there. Lucas, Sari, and Randy will be our power line. Mike, you play defense with Felipe. Remember, guys, keep passing the puck until you get a good shot. Then take it!"

Sari won the face-off again and sent the puck back to me. I passed it over to Felipe. Then he passed it to Lucas.

Sari had worked her way in front of the Penguin goal again.

"Lucas! Lucas!" she yelled. She was wide open.

Lucas passed back to Felipe.

"Give it to Sari!" I screamed.

But Felipe passed it to me instead. I tried to get the puck to Sari, but I didn't have a clear lane. A Penguin blocked the pass. He sent the puck all the way down to our end of the ice.

By the time Sari grabbed the puck back, she couldn't get near the goal. So she passed the puck to Lucas. He took a quick shot. The Penguin goalie blocked it. Felipe swooped in and stole the puck. Sari was open, but Felipe didn't pass to her.

Then I knew it for sure. Felipe wasn't

ever going to pass to Sari. No matter what.

The Penguins' penalty ended without us scoring.

When we skated off the ice, Mr. Slocum was steamed.

"What's going on out there?" he yelled at Lucas and Felipe.

"We didn't have a good shot," Lucas said. He wouldn't look at Mr. Slocum. I knew it was because he was lying.

"If I didn't know better," Mr. Slocum said, "I might think you were keeping the puck away from one of our players. But no North Star would do that." Mr. Slocum stomped down to the other side of the bench.

Then we heard a loud cheer from the Penguins' bench. They had just tied the game.

That gave the Penguins the lift they needed. They scored two more goals really fast. Meanwhile, the North Stars just couldn't work together as a team. Felipe wouldn't pass to Sari. And now Sari wouldn't pass to him.

The second and third periods were a disaster. We looked as if we were playing our very first game. We were down 7–4.

Then something amazing happened. Cliff scored a goal! It was the first one he had ever scored in a real game. Everyone went crazy. Cliff had a big, goofy smile on his face. The referee told him he could keep the puck because it was his first goal.

About thirty seconds later, Lucas and Teddy executed a perfect give-and-go that ended in a score. Now we were only one goal behind.

The Penguins looked scared. They knew we could come back and win. We were on a roll!

There was only about a minute left in the game. Mr. Slocum sent Sari, Lucas, and Randy out as a line, with Felipe and Cliff as defense.

"Come on, North Stars," Mr. Slocum yelled. "It's ours to win!"

The Penguins won the face-off. But Randy stole the puck back. He skated down the left side of the ice. Lucas and Sari were right behind him.

The game clock showed thirty-two seconds left.

Randy passed the puck to Sari. The Penguin goalie knew she could score, and moved toward her.

Now the whole left side of their goal was open. That's when Lucas came flying in. The goalie didn't see him. One pass from Sari, and Lucas would tie the game.

We all saw Sari look right at Lucas. But she didn't pass to him! She tried to send the puck back to Randy instead. One of the Penguins knocked it away. The buzzer sounded. We lost. Again.

"Are you blind?" Lucas screamed at Sari. "I was wide open."

"Me blind? How about you?" Sari shouted back. "I've been open all night, and you didn't pass to me once!"

Mr. Slocum told them to calm down, but they kept on yelling. They were yelling while we shook hands with the Penguins. I think I heard them yelling all the way to the parking lot.

I wasn't looking forward to the next practice.

But then it turned out there might not be a next practice.

Steve Slocum called me at home that night with the bad news. "My dad fell off a ladder and broke his leg," he wailed. "The doctor told him to stay off it for at least *eight* weeks. He feels really bad. He can't be our coach anymore!"

I was in shock when I hung up the phone.

We truly were the No Stars. No wins. No teamwork. No coach.

And maybe—no team.

Don't Quit Your Day Job, Dad!

We were in big trouble. The North Stars couldn't play any games unless we had a coach. We couldn't even have a practice. That was the league rule.

We had to find a new coach—fast!

The next afternoon we had an emergency meeting at the rink. Just us guys.

"My dad hates the cold," Felipe explained. "He wears about six layers of clothes whenever he comes to a game. No way he's going to come here for practices. Plus, he doesn't even know how to skate."

"How about Cliff's dad?" Teddy asked.

"He's really cool."

"He's cool, but he's a doctor," Cliff said. "He's always getting called to the hospital. He couldn't coach us. He might have to go deliver a baby in the middle of a game or something."

"What about your dad, Ted?" Felipe asked.

"He's already coaching my sister's basketball team," Teddy said with a sigh.

"How about your father, Mike?" Felipe asked.

"I don't know," I said. "He's never coached anything. And I know he never played hockey."

"Mike, you've got to ask him. He's our last chance," Teddy said. He put his arm around my shoulder. "We're counting on you to talk him into it."

"I'll try," I mumbled. The team always seemed to be counting on me for something.

I had to pick just the right moment to approach my dad. That's how it works best. I lucked out, because my mom brought home a pizza that night. My dad loves pizza. I knew he'd be in a good mood at dinner.

I waited until Dad took his first bite.

"Mmm, that's good," he said.

"Dad," I began. "I have to ask you something very important." He glanced at me. I decided I had better get it all out at once. "We really, *really* need a coach. Would you coach us? Please?"

"Huh? What did you say?"

Maybe I blurted it out too fast.

"My hockey team, Dad," I said more slowly. "We need a coach. Mr. Slocum broke his leg. He had to quit."

"That's too bad, Mike. But I don't think I'd be a very good coach." He put down his slice. "I love coming to your games and watching you play. But I still don't understand all the rules. And you've been playing for the Mets for three years now."

Typical Dad. The Mets are my Little League team. I didn't even bother to correct him. I'm used to it. My dad can tell you who won some crazy war in 1591, but he has trouble remembering what color our car is.

"Dad, you don't have to know the rules. *We* all know them. We just need a grown-up to run practice and be at the games. Otherwise, we can't play. Anyhow, I bet coaching is a lot like being a teacher." I'm glad I thought of that last point. My dad is a high school history teacher, and he loves teaching.

"Mike," my dad said, "can't someone else's father do it? I'm the wrong person for the job. I'm just not a sports kind of guy."

"No. We've tried everyone," I told him. "You're our last hope."

"How can you refuse a request like that?" my mother asked with a laugh. "Come on, Howard. Give it a try."

"Yeah, Dad. Just try it." I got down on my knees by the kitchen table. I held up my hands as if I were praying. "Puhh-leeesse. I'm begging you."

Now my dad started laughing. "No fair. You guys are ganging up on me! I know—why don't you do it, honey?" he asked my mom. He picked up his slice.

"Come on, Dad. Be serious," I said.

I could tell my father was thinking it over. A big piece of cheese slid off his pizza and fell on the table. He didn't even notice it.

"Okay—" he began.

"Great!" I jumped up off the floor.

"Wait, Mike, listen. We'll give it a try," my dad said. "I'll coach the next practice. We'll see how it goes. Then we'll decide if it's working. If it's not, you find someone else. Is that a deal?"

"Thank you, Dad. Thank you, thank you, thank you!" I gave him a big hug. Then I ran to call Teddy with the good news. We still had a girl on the team, but at least we had a coach. One problem down, one to go.

I knew we were in trouble when my dad showed up at practice with a book he had borrowed from the library. I hoped none of the guys would notice that the title was *Anyone Can Coach Hockey.*

My dad spent most of the practice standing by our bench, his nose in the book. Every now and then he would yell things at us. "Okay. Time for passing drills. . . . No, we already did that.

"How about skating backward? Oh, that's what you're doing now."

We finally got a practice game going, but Dad kept forgetting to change lines.

By the end of practice, everyone was fooling around on the ice. Some guys were playing tag. Randy and Brendan were squirting each other with the goalies' water bottles. Even Teddy was goofing off. But my dad kept smiling and reading the book.

"Nice pass, Randy. Good shot, Lucas!" he would shout out every now and then.

"You're getting much better, Cliff," he said, just as Cliff skated backward into Steve. They both fell into the goal.

When practice was over, I told my dad I was going to walk home with Felipe. I wanted to see what Felipe thought about him. Dad wasn't a good coach. But he was all we had.

By the time I made it outside, everyone had left. Felipe must have decided to go with someone else. I had this horrible feeling that right now the whole team was laughing about my dad.

I walked about two blocks, and then I saw someone a little ahead of me. She had a hockey stick over her shoulder. I knew it had to be Sari.

Before I could run, she turned and saw me.

"Hi, Mike," she called.

"Hi, Sari." I had to say something, right?

"Your dad's nice," she said, waiting for me to catch up.

"Thanks. He *is* nice. He's just not a very good coach," I said. "Is he?"

Sari laughed. But it wasn't a mean laugh. "No, he's not. He's pretty bad," she said. "But he's nice."

I started laughing too. I had to admit it. He was terrible. But at least Sari seemed to like him anyway. And she wasn't going to make fun of him.

But we still had a big problem. "What are we going to do?" I said. "If we don't have a coach, we can't play. But if my dad coaches us, we're going to lose."

Sari brushed her hair back from her face. I noticed that she had little freckles across her nose and nice teeth. No braces.

"You're right. We really do need a different coach," Sari agreed. She sighed.

Then her whole face lit up. "And I know the perfect person!" she said. "A great skater. Knows a lot about hockey. Likes kids. And even has some free time!" She had a big smile on her face.

"That's great!" I said. "When can he start?"

"Right away." Then Sari's grin became so big her nose crinkled up. "There's just one thing. Some of the guys are going to totally hate this. I'll only get us the new coach if you go along with the idea."

Sari quickly told me her plan. She was right. The guys were going to go nuts when they found out.

But it was our only hope.

Can You Say "Coach Janet"?

The next night at practice, we had a new coach.

Sari Baxter's mom.

"Who's that?" Lucas asked. He rubbed his eyes as if he couldn't believe what he was seeing.

"Our new coach," I said.

"What do you mean?" asked Teddy. "What happened to your dad?"

"He fired himself," I replied. It was true. As soon as I got home, my dad told me he had already returned his book to the library. I guess not everyone can coach hockey. My dad was proof!

"Oh, noooo," Lucas groaned.

"Wait, Lucas. Don't freak out yet. We're really lucky. Mrs. Baxter knows a lot about hockey." I hoped the guys would give her a chance. And not get mad at me for thinking Mrs. Baxter was a good idea.

"Sari's dad played in college," I continued, "so Mrs. Baxter's been to lots of games."

"So why doesn't her *dad* coach us?" Felipe asked.

"Yeah, what about him?" Steve demanded.

"He can't. He's a policeman. He works nights a lot," I explained. "Sari's mom will be great. She definitely knows more about hockey than my dad. More than your dad, too, I bet."

"No way," Steve said.

"This is too much," Lucas said. "First, a girl on the team. Now a girl for a coach.

What's next? Gorilla goalies?"

"Chill out, Lucas," I said. "Sari says her mom used to be a professional figure skater. She was even in ice shows. And she's not a girl. She's a mom!"

"Figure skating? What's that got to do with hockey?" Steve sneered.

"Sari says her mom can teach us to skate faster," I replied. "And stop and turn better too."

"Sari says! Sari says!" Lucas shouted. "What's going on here, Mike? All of a sudden Sari Baxter is your new best friend?"

"Of course not," I said. "I just want to play hockey. And maybe win once in a while."

"Well, there's no way I'm playing for a lady coach," Lucas shot back. "I'm going on strike. I'll just sit here and watch you guys. And laugh."

"I'm with Lucas," Felipe said. "I'm on strike too."

"You guys are acting crazy," I said. I finished lacing my skates. Then I grabbed my stick and stepped out onto the ice. Sari was the only other North Star out there.

The two of us skated around, warming up. One by one I noticed the other North Stars come in. They each stared at Mrs. Baxter, in her blue jeans and her MAINE HOCKEY sweatshirt. Then they sat on the bench with Lucas and Felipe. Not even Teddy or Randy came out with us. They were all on strike!

Sari's mom just kept making notes on her clipboard. Every once in a while she looked over at the bench. Once I saw her counting the number of players. Finally, Cliff walked in. He was the last guy.

Then Mrs. Baxter blew her whistle.

"Okay, let's get started," she called. "Sari, Mike, sit down with the rest of the team."

While we hurried over to the bench,

Mrs. Baxter skated around the rink. She had on real hockey skates and skated just like Sari. They both had smooth, strong strokes. They were both fast and powerful. I wished the guys could see how good they were.

Mrs. Baxter finished her lap around the rink with a sharp stop in front of the bench. A huge spray of ice flew up and over us. She gave a little smile when we all ducked.

"I'm Janet Baxter. You've probably guessed that I'm your new coach. And I'm sure you know that I'm also Sari's mother."

No one said anything. Everyone stared straight ahead.

Mrs. Baxter was still smiling. "I have a feeling that something is bothering you guys," she said. "Anyone care to tell me what's going on?"

Silence.

I looked down at the ground. I felt bad

for her. And I felt even worse that the North Stars were going to blow their last shot at a coach. Which would mean we wouldn't be able to play anymore.

Finally, Felipe cleared his throat as if he were going to say something.

"You're Felipe, right?" Mrs. Baxter said. "Can you tell me what's going on?"

"Yeah. We're on strike. I mean, we feel kind of...well, weird, having a lady coach."

"Yeah," Lucas piped up. "The other teams already make fun of us because we have a girl on the team."

"I thought that might be the problem," Mrs. Baxter said. At least she didn't seem mad.

"So we're leaving now," Felipe said. Then he looked over at me. "All of us."

He and Lucas picked up their sticks and skates and started toward the door. After a couple of seconds, Randy, Tommy, Steve, and the rest of the team stood up to leave. Everyone but me and Sari. What jerks!

"Wait!" Mrs. Baxter shouted. "I'll give you a fair chance to get rid of me—with no hard feelings. We'll make it a bet."

Mrs. Baxter grinned. I glanced over at Sari. She seemed as surprised as everyone else.

"Here's the bet. I'll race each of you the length of the rink. If anyone beats me—I'll quit. But if I win each race, I get to coach for the rest of the season."

"Let me get this straight," Lucas said. "If just one of us beats you, you'll quit?"

"That's right." Mrs. Baxter nodded, her fluffy blond hair bouncing up and down. "But if I win, you'll play for me all season. No quitting. No strikes. And *no* attitude."

Felipe and Lucas glanced at each other. Felipe nodded to Lucas.

"You've got a bet, Mrs. Baxter."

"There's no way she can beat all of us," Felipe said. "That's fourteen races in a row!" He and Lucas slapped high-fives.

Mrs. Baxter blew her whistle. She looked pleased.

"Okay, gang," she said. "Here are the rules. We start here at this goal and race down to the other end of the rink. We go around that goal and then back here. First one back wins."

Teddy and Felipe snickered.

"Now, who's my first victim?" She

tossed the clipboard onto the bench. No one answered. We all looked at each other, waiting for someone to volunteer.

Mrs. Baxter just stood there, smiling. She didn't seem nervous at all.

"I'll go first, I guess," Steve said. He unbuckled his goalie leg pads. Mrs. Baxter wouldn't have any trouble beating him. Steve wasn't a very good skater. That was one reason he became a goalie in the first place. Of course, he wasn't much of a goalie either.

Steve and Mrs. Baxter lined up next to the goal. "Lucas, why don't you start us?" Mrs. Baxter said. She threw Lucas her whistle.

Lucas grabbed it and nodded. Then he blew the whistle and Steve and Mrs. Baxter took off. After about four strokes, she was way in front of Steve. She took it easy—and she still beat him by almost half the length of the rink.

"She's smart," Felipe whispered to me "She's not letting herself get tired out."

Tommy went next. Even though he was a lot faster than Steve, Mrs. Baxter finished at least five yards ahead of him.

Lucas suddenly pushed Sari to the front.

"I'm not racing," Sari announced. "I know my mom can beat me. Anyhow, I *want* her to be our coach."

"Oh, no," Lucas said. "The bet is that your mom races all of us. And if you don't race her, we win."

"Lucas is right," Mrs. Baxter said. "That's the bet."

Sari shrugged and got into position. "And no taking it easy, either," Felipe said.

Sari turned on Felipe in a flash. "Don't worry about me," she snapped. "I always play to win."

Lucas blew the whistle. Sari took off fast and hard.

She and her mom were neck and neck all the way up to the other goal. The rink was totally silent. All we could hear was their skates scraping on the ice.

They started back toward us. I could see from the serious look on Sari's face that she really was trying to win. Even if it meant beating her mom.

Then Mrs. Baxter slowly began to pull away from Sari. We could see Sari straining to catch up. Her face was red. She was swinging her arms back and forth to help her skate faster. But Sari finished about two feet behind her mother.

Sari was so tired she couldn't stand up straight. She put her hands on her knees. Then she bent over, trying to catch her breath.

"You all right, Sari?" Mrs. Baxter called.

Sari nodded her head. She couldn't even answer.

Lucas stared at her. Then he skated over and took Steve's water bottle off the top of the goal. He handed it to Sari.

"Nice race," I heard him say. "I thought you might beat her."

"Thanks," Sari gasped. She took a big drink of water. "I've never beaten her yet. But I will someday."

Randy skated next. Then Cliff and Tommy. Nobody came anywhere as close as Sari had. Not even Lucas.

Then it was my turn.

"Ready, Mrs. Baxter?" Lucas asked.

She just nodded her head. I glanced over at her. Mrs. Baxter wiped the sweat off her forehead with her sleeve. But she still didn't look tired.

Lucas blew the whistle. I took off. After about twenty-five feet, I knew I didn't have a chance.

Mrs. Baxter had a good lead on me when we rounded the far goal. But suddenly, one of her skates slipped sideways on the ice. She nearly fell down.

I was ahead of her before I knew what was happening. I could hear everyone screaming. "Go, Mike! Go! Go! Go!"

I couldn't help myself. I skated as hard as I could, even though I knew that if I won, the No Stars wouldn't have a coach.

The finish line was only about ten feet away. I realized I was going to win!

That's when Mrs. Baxter flashed by me on my right. She was the winner. But only by inches.

I couldn't stand up at all. My legs were jelly. I leaned against the boards. Sari came over with the water bottle.

"That was incredible," she said. "I thought you were going to win for sure."

"Thanks," I said. I took a drink. The water tasted so good. Mrs. Baxter was about fifteen feet away, leaning against the boards. Suddenly, she looked really tired.

"You better give your mom some of this," I said to Sari. "She looks like she needs it."

Sari took the water bottle over to her mom. I was worried. Maybe I shouldn't have skated so hard.

There was only one race left. But it was with Felipe.

Our fastest skater.

Felipe took his place at the starting line.

"This is it!" Lucas announced. "The last race."

Mrs. Baxter pushed herself away from the boards and lined up beside Felipe. She bent over, took a deep breath, and then nodded to Lucas.

"On your mark," Lucas shouted. Then he blew the whistle.

Felipe was in the lead right from the start. We could all see that Sari's mom was really tired. She just didn't have any energy left. When they went around the other goal, Mrs. Baxter looked as if she were going to fall.

Felipe skated with smooth steady strides. Mrs. Baxter was working hard.

I glanced over at Sari. She had a worried expression on her face. "Come on, Mom!" she shouted.

"Go for it, Mrs. B.!" I heard someone shout. I turned around and almost fell off my skates. It was Lucas!

"You can do it, Mrs. B.!" Now Randy was shouting. Then we all started cheering Mrs. Baxter.

She must have heard us, because that's when she started to catch up with Felipe. He heard her coming. He crouched deeper, skating harder. But she kept gaining on him.

Now they were only about thirty feet away from the finish line. Mrs. Baxter still hadn't passed Felipe. It looked as if she might have waited too long.

"Go! Go! Go!" We all screamed at the top of our lungs. And we were screaming for the lady coach. I wondered for a second if that would make Felipe mad.

Felipe still had the lead with only a few feet left. Then Mrs. Baxter hurled herself through the air toward the finish line. Her arms were stretched out in front of her. She looked as if she were flying. She glided across the finish line with Felipe. They were only about an inch apart. My heart sank. From where I was standing, it looked as if Felipe crossed first.

Mrs. Baxter stopped next to the wall. She was breathing really hard and her face was pink and covered in sweat. She bent over with her hands on her knees.

Sari raced over to her. "Mom, are you okay?" she cried.

"Yeah, I'm fine. What a race!" Mrs. Baxter slowly straightened up. "Who won?"

I didn't want to be the one to say that Felipe had beaten her. So I looked over at Lucas. But Felipe answered first.

"You won," Felipe said. "It was close, but you just got by me."

I couldn't believe it! Felipe had to know that he had won! What was going on?

"Nice race, Felipe," Mrs. Baxter said. She skated over and put out her hand.

"Nice race...Coach," Felipe said. Felipe and Mrs. Baxter shook hands. The whole team went nuts cheering. Even Sari and Lucas slapped high-fives.

"Coach! Coach! Coach!" Teddy started chanting. We all took up the cheer and skated in a big circle around Mrs. Baxter. *Coach* Baxter. She was laughing and shaking her head.

"I'm going to take a five-minute break," she said with a laugh. "Then we'll finish practice."

We all streamed out onto the ice. Steve

strapped his goalie pads back on. Someone threw a bunch of pucks on the ice. I saw Felipe and Sari talking. I don't know what they said, but I guess they made up, because they started passing the puck back and forth.

Coach Baxter blew her whistle.

"Back to work, team!" she shouted. She seemed okay now. "We have only twenty minutes left. We've got a game with the Black Hawks on Friday, and we're going to be ready."

She took a long look at us.

"I know some of the other teams have been teasing you, calling you the No Stars. But you know, that's actually a *good* name. A name to be proud of. That's because there are no *stars* here. Just one solid team!

"So let's get going, No Stars!" She blew her whistle again, and the guys all cheered. I smiled. Coach Baxter didn t call us "men."

Yup. Things were definitely looking up.

ALWAYS USE A STICK THAT'S THE RIGHT SIZE

Be sure your stick is the right length. Otherwise, you will have lots of trouble making and receiving passes and taking shots.

The end of your stick should just reach your chin when you are wearing skates.

If your stick is too long, ask your mom, dad, or coach to cut it down. If it's too short, it's time to buy a new stick!

SKATING WITH THE PUCK

Always keep the puck in front of you. Don't drag it along next to you. Move the puck ahead using the blade of your stick.

Here are a couple of hints to help you control the puck: Keep both of your hands on the stick. And always keep your head up—otherwise you won't see the other skaters, and you'll get checked off the puck before you know it!

Jim O'Connor is the author of many books for children. Recent titles include *Shadow Ball: The History of the Negro Leagues, Jackie Robinson and the Story of All-Black Baseball, The Ghost in Tent 19,* and *Slime Time,* all published by Random House.

Jim was raised in upstate New York, where he learned to ski and ice-skate at an early age. He never played organized hockey, but he enjoyed playing lots of "disorganized" hockey outdoors during the long, cold winters. Jim's other favorite sport is long-distance running. One of his greatest thrills was finishing the New York City Marathon.

Jim lives in New York City with his wife, Jane, and their sons, Robby and Teddy.

Don't miss the next book in the No Stars series:

#2: The Puck Stops Here!

"This Wayne guy better be good," Teddy snapped. "Playing street hockey isn't the same as..."

"Wayne will be great," Sari interrupted. "He'll be an awesome goalie. Just because he's not one of your buddies doesn't mean he stinks."

"Why don't I know him?" I asked.

"Because Wayne's a year younger than us," Sari explained. "He's in the third grade."

"Whoa, whoa, whoa!" Teddy shook his head. "You think your *third-grade pal* can just walk onto our team?" he sneered. "Just like that!"

"He's probably better than a couple of your fourth-grade pals," Sari said. "Just give him a chance!"

I just kept thinking about Wayne.

A third-grader.

Who had only played street hockey.

The No Stars were having their usual lousy luck.

I mean, how good could this kid be?